Little Banty Chicken
and the Big Dream

Lynea Gillen

Illustrated by Kristina Swarner

Three Pebble Press, LLC
Portland, Oregon

Printed in Korea

ISBN: 978-0-9960219-1-3
ISBN: 978-0-9960219-2-0 (ebook)

Three Pebble Press, LLC
10040 SW 25th Ave
Portland, OR 97219-6325 U.S.A.

ThreePebblePress.com

Volume discounts available.

Layout Design by paisleyarts.com

Editing by Geo Grant

Gillen, Lynea.
   Little Banty Chicken and the big dream / Lynea Gillen ; illustrated by
Kristina Swarner.

   pages : color illustrations ; cm

   Summary: "An enchanting tale of one little chicken who has the courage
to make her dream come true with the support of the wise moon and her
barnyard friends ... Activity sheets inspire children to identify and share
their dreams, work together to help others, and celebrate life."--Provided by
publisher.
   Interest age level: 003-008.
   Issued also as an ebook.
   ISBN: 978-0-9960219-1-3

   1. Chickens--Juvenile fiction. 2. Goal (Psychology)--Juvenile fiction. 3.
Helping behavior--Juvenile fiction. 4. Chickens--Fiction. 5. Goal (Psychology)-
-Fiction. 6. Helpfulness--Fiction. I. Swarner, Kristina. II. Title.

PZ7.G55 Li 2016
[E]

To Anna and Jim

Little Banty Chicken
loved to dream.
At night, when the other
chickens and animals
were sleeping, Little Banty
would stroll out into the
big open field, and look up
at the stars and Moon.
She had many big dreams
and she told Moon
all about them.

One night she was out under the stars
and she told Moon about one of her dreams.

"I dream of having a beautiful party for the Farmers,"
Little Banty told Moon. "It would be a summer night
celebration under the stars. There would be big
bowls of vegetables from all over the farm, and all
the animals and the Farmer family would come
together to eat, dance and sing. You would
be there Moon, shining down on all of us."

"That's a wonderful dream," Moon said to Little Banty.
"I can see it in my imagination."

Night after night, Little Banty
would go out into the field
and tell Moon about her
dream of the big party.
The more she talked about it,
the bigger the dream became.

One night, Moon said, "Little Banty,
if you want to make your dream
come true, you should share
it with others."

"Oh, no," Little Banty said. "They will
laugh at me and tell me that the dream
is too big for such a little chicken!"

"Maybe you can start with one friend,"
Moon gently said. "Do you have
one friend who might like
to hear about your dream?"

Little Banty thought of Squirrel.
She was very friendly and always listened to Little Banty.
Maybe she could tell Squirrel about her dream.

So the next day, Little Banty found Squirrel.
She was a little nervous to tell her
and she thought she might need Moon's help.

"Squirrel," Little Banty said, "Do you want to come
and dream with me under the stars and Moon tonight?"
Little Banty's eyes sparkled when she told Squirrel.
Squirrel thought it was an exciting idea.

That night, Squirrel joined Little Banty
under the stars and Moon.

Little Banty looked up at Moon for courage,
then she told Squirrel about her dream of a magical
celebration for the Farmers under the stars.

"That's a wonderful dream!" exclaimed Squirrel.
"I can imagine it! Can I bring a bowl of hazelnuts?"

"Mmmm! Fresh hazelnuts!" Little Banty said.
"Yes, please!"

"Let's tell Cow!" said Squirrel.
Little Banty looked up at Moon. Moon smiled.

The next day, Squirrel and Little Banty
strolled up to Cow, and Squirrel invited her
to join them under the stars and Moon.
That night, Little Banty told Cow her dream
of the magical party.

"That's a wonderful dream!" exclaimed Cow.
"I can bring sweet cream!"

"Yes, please!" Little Banty said.
"I love sweet cream!"

"Let's tell Horse!" Cow said.

So the next day, Little Banty, Squirrel and Cow
went out into the big open field. They found Horse, and
Cow invited him to join them under the stars and Moon.

That night, Little Banty shared her dream with Horse.

"That's a wonderful dream!" exclaimed Horse. "I can
use my cart to bring food from the country store."

"Yes, please!" Little Banty said. "You can bring
fresh peaches from the store. They will taste
so good with the sweet cream!"

Each night the dream got bigger and bigger,
with more animals, food and dancing.

Little Banty invited Magpie.
"I can tell stories!" she called.

"Yes, you are a wonderful storyteller, Magpie,"
Little Banty said.

"We should invite Rabbit and
the Song Sparrows!" Magpie said.

So, Rabbit and the Song Sparrows
joined them under Moon and the stars.

Rabbit said, "I can bring fresh vegetables
from the garden!"

The Song Sparrows said, "We can sing for the party."

"Let's invite Cat and Dog!" Rabbit said.

"This is going to be a magical celebration!"
Little Banty said.

The next night, Cat and Dog
joined the group.

Cat and Dog loved the idea of having
a special party for the Farmers.
Since Cat and Dog lived in the
Farmers' house, they could help
make the party a surprise.
"We can tell you when the Farmers
are away so we can plan
the party!" Dog said.

Then Moon said,
"Let's have the party on a night when
I am full and can light up the sky!"

The day of the party finally arrived.
The Farmers drove into town for an afternoon
of shopping, and the animals all worked
together to set the table and prepare
for the celebration.

Moon was just coming up
when the Farmers arrived home.
Dog started barking.

"What is it?" asked Mother.

Anna and Jimmy, the two Farmer
children, decided to follow Dog outside.
They ran to the table where all
the animals were waiting.
Anna and Jimmy were surprised
and delighted! They ran to get
Father and Mother.

"Surprise!" exclaimed all the animals.

Father, Mother, Anna and Jimmy could hardly believe their eyes! Moon was shining brightly, the Song Sparrows were singing, and all around the table were their beloved animals. The table was decorated with flowers, food and gifts from the garden.

And Little Banty had the biggest smile anyone had ever seen on a chicken!

That night
there was a great
celebration with dancing,
singing and storytelling.
The animals told the Farmers
about dreaming under the stars and Moon.
Moon told them how Little Banty Chicken
had shared her dream many moons
ago and how each animal had helped
in planning the celebration.

The Farmers went to bed that
night with hearts full of love.

After the celebration, all the
animals met under Moon and
the stars to talk about the party.
Then they heard rustling in the bushes.

Little Banty looked up and there stood Anna and Jimmy.

"We have a dream," Anna said shyly.

"Oh! Come join us!" said Little Banty Chicken.
"We would love to hear your dream!"

So Anna and Jimmy joined the animals
under the stars and Moon and
they shared their dream.
Moon and all the animals listened.

"What a wonderful dream!"
Little Banty said,
"I can see it in my imagination!"

All the animals nodded. Moon smiled.

I wonder what the
children dreamed.

Do you know?

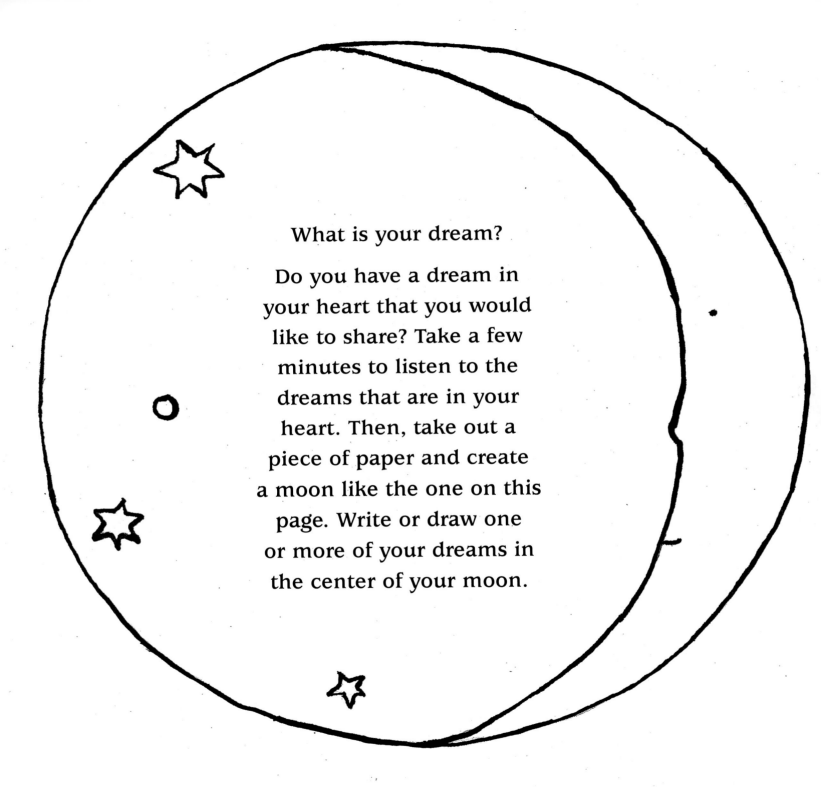

What is your dream?

Do you have a dream in your heart that you would like to share? Take a few minutes to listen to the dreams that are in your heart. Then, take out a piece of paper and create a moon like the one on this page. Write or draw one or more of your dreams in the center of your moon.

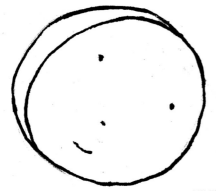

Who are the people in
your life who can listen
to your dreams?

Think of the friends
and family members
in your life. Then, take
out a piece of paper
and write the names
of the people who will
help you make your
dreams come true.

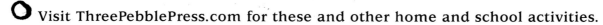

Lynea Gillen, LPC, MS, has been sharing her love of literature with children for over 30 years as a school teacher and counselor. Now in private practice, she is the creator of the highly regarded Mindful Moments Cards, as well as three *Mom's Choice Award* winners: the illustrated children's book *Good People Everywhere*, book *Yoga Calm for Children* and DVD *Kids Teach Yoga: Flying Eagle*. Lynea lives in Portland, Oregon, with her husband Jim, where she enjoys hiking, gardening and spending time dreaming big with her granddaughter Anna.

Kristina Swarner is an award-winning illustrator (Sydney Taylor Book Award) whose numerous books include *Good People Everywhere*, *Before You Were Born* and *Enchanted Lions*. Using imagery and inspiration from memories of exploring old houses, woods and gardens as a child, her work is often described as "magical" and "dreamlike." When not painting, Kristina enjoys music, reading and trying to grow trees on her balcony. She lives in Chicago.

Other Family and School Resources from Lynea Gillen

Good People Everywhere
A soothing story to help children become mindful of the beautiful, caring people in their world.

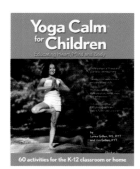

Yoga Calm for Children: Educating Heart, Mind and Body
Help children develop self-control, attention, fitness and social/emotional skills with this award-winning book.

Mindful Moments Cards
Short contemplations that develop imagination, attention, relaxation skills and positive feelings.

Order these and other products at ThreePebblePress.com.